Ava's Journey

CW00840248

Chapter One

Ava Nelsen opened her Bible

and turned to the book of John and

read the whole book before leaving

the church that Sunday. Her life

hadn't always been filled with

people who loved her or spending

time with God but things had

changed in her short life time.

Her mom and dad had given her

up at the age of five but she had

been adopted at the age of six. But

sometimes she wondered if she

really belonged with them.

She longed to see her real mom

again. Why after all of this time?

She wondered that and felt bad

every time she talked to her

adopted mom about it. She always

had a look of sadness on her face.
And yesterday was no different
when she brought it up. But as she
was leaving for college soon she
really wanted to make things right
before then.

She walked home from church
where her parents as a child used
to take her and she had always
continued since giving her life over
to Jesus.

But her adopted family did not
believe or want anything to do with

God. She prayed for them every day that they would see the truth but loved them all anyway. She was thankful for the love that they showed her. For no one had ever loved her like they had.

"I'll bring you if you want. Your mom probably won't want to go with. She'll be too emotional", her dad told her as she walked in the door.

She nodded and then headed to do some last minute packing before leaving. She looked around her room one last time and laughed when she noticed her stuffed animals still on her bed after all these years.

Ava walked in the kitchen and noticed her mom doing the dishes and she almost burst into tears right there.

Saying good bye would not be easy. She had to admit more than ever before that she was her mom and no one could really ever take her place. She had fed, clothed, loved, and been there for her more than any real mom ever could. She was who she was now saying good bye to. And would miss more than ever.

"You could just stay home and be here forever, that would be fine with me", she said, as she wiped her forehead of her baking and she had done earlier.

Ava couldn't even remember a time where her mom wasn't

working. She loved her she knew but she was also really busy. Doing something or being there for someone. Sometimes Ava wished that she had had an easier life.

And she wished that she had gone to God more and not burdened her mom with the things she went through.

But as she hugged her good bye she knew that she would be there for her future children just as much.

"If I stayed here you would get tired of me but wouldn't let me know. I know you", Ava said, and wiped away a tear. She knew that she might not live there again and it brought her a certain sadness.

"That's not true...I would let you know", her mom teased, and then laughed like she did when she was certain she was really funny even if no one else did. But Ava would miss her sense of humour.

"Ha ha. Very funny. Bye mom",
she said, giving her a hug. She
hugged her daughter and then
went back to work.

Ava watched her and then left
with her last bit of luggage. She
went to the car and opened the
door and the drive to school was a
day's drive.

But she was thankful that she
had her dad to bring her because
otherwise she might just end up
going back home. He was always

the one to encourage her to out and be one her own and know was no different.

"I think it's just time", he said, as they neared the school.

"I know your mother doesn't think so though, but you have to do what's best for you", he said, "I know you'll make friends and have fun"

"What's best for me...", Ava repeated. How often she had heard those words and lived by them. She always had thought about herself and what was really best for her. But what if God wanted her to be there for someone else and it didn't always seem to be best for her?

"Here you are, have fun, and we'll come visit you soon. You are after all eighteen. Time to spread your wings and fly the nest"

Ava looked at her dad and sighed. She wasn't quite sure if she was ready for this yet. She still wanted to be at home where things were comfortable and she knew what to expect. Here she was alone and vulnerable and knew no one.

"I'll help you get your things inside", he said, and brought her suitcases to her dorm room. Then he hugged her good bye and left her alone.

On her bed. Lost in her thoughts. Lost in a daze. She wanted to run back and go home with him. She wanted to be home where he was. Sure it was good to be on her own and doing her own thing but she wanted to be with her father.

Then she smiled thinking about how that was kind of similar to how she thought of God. Sure it was good being on the earth and having freedom to do what she wanted.

But really she wanted be with her God. To walk with him and spend time with her heavenly father. But she wanted to do his purpose for her here on earth first.

To live for him, happily and healthily. And wait on his timing. What better timing was there than that?

Feeling filled with his love and life she went for a walk down the sidewalk and passed by the different stores in that small town. Already she loved it there.

And she hoped that wouldn't go away any time soon.

Chapter Two

Ava sat on her bed the next day and waited for her roommate to come. She still wasn't there yet and she was wondering where she was staying.

Ava headed to where the chapel was and opened the door, walking into the sanctuary.

She heard people playing music and she took a seat in the back listening to them playing there worship music and suddenly she knew that this was where she was supposed to be.

In the presence of such worship. What could really take God's place? She had worked at home and that was great, but she knew that sometimes it was nice to just be in the Holy Spirits presence.

Not that he wasn't in her wherever she went, she realized then. He was always with her no matter where she went. Because he lived inside her.

"You with the band?", one of the guys nearby asked her.

"Nope, just thought I would listen in", she said then as he was about to ask her to leave.

When one of the guys in the band spoke up, "hey if she can sing she should join us. We need another girl voice. You up for it?"

Ava laughed at first and then agreed. Next she was on stage and singing into a microphone. The guy that had wanted to kick her out looked annoyed but she was happier than she had been in a long time.

She smiled at the guy that had invited her and then kept singing for God. She knew there were many reasons to be sad right then but she wanted to praise her father in heaven more than ever.

She sang loudly and then when practice was over the guy who invited her onto stage soon left with another girl.

They looked happy and in love and she had to admit that having that would be nice.

But she didn't want to focus on that too much that year and wanted to have that year be about

God, and a year of studying hard at the Christian University.

"He's been dating her for years now", another guy in the group told her, "they're engaged"

Ava thought something was wrong with her that she was already disappointed. Already he was engaged. She wondered then why he was so wanting her to come on stage with them.

"He sure makes a girl feel welcome", she said, trying to hide her disappointment.

"That's him. That's actually how he and Pricilla started out too. She was a part of the band but for some reason she dropped out. Too bad. We sounded really good with her apart of things"

Ava looked at him like he was maybe hiding something now. They both just sighed and then laughed when they looked at each other.

"So you coming to practice then? It's on Thursday. Every Thursday and we sing at most chapels in the morning leading worship and every Sunday.

I know it's a big commitment but it's so good to do. You in?", the guy said and then Ava realized that she didn't even know his name.

"Yeah, sure. I mean, I think so. I just might have too much school work to do. But I would love to. I used to lead worship in my church at home sometimes", she told him, "and I still don't know your name"

"It's Phillip. But most people call me Phil. You can do what you want. See you on Thursday then", he said, friendly.

Ava laughed as he just assumed that she was going to do it. But she guessed that he was probably right. She wanted to do something to not be so homesick and she thought worshipping God would do just that.

"Oh I forgot my papers for next Sunday", the guy from earlier said, as he came back and Ava tried to hide her smile. She did not want to fall for someone that was taken and be heartbroken later on.

"I didn't get your name", he asked her, finding the papers and then looking like he would leave soon.

"It's Ava", she said nervously, "and you are?"

"David. You sounded really good today by the way. Ever since

Pricilla dropped out we've been needing another girl singer and you were just the one. See you Thursday?", he said, eying her.

"Sure. Phillip already filled me in on everything to do with all the practices and he also let me know too all about your wedding. But that's exciting. And you've been dating awhile now?"

He stopped and took a seat on one of the benches. Then he looked up at her like he had the weight of the world on his shoulders. What was going on with him that she didn't know?

"Yes, we've been together for four years now. I thought we were good together but...it's complicated. But I don't want to bore you with it all"

"You can tell me. I can keep secrets that's for sure", she said, but then wondered if it was such a good idea when she was biased already.

"Well when I went on a mission's trip there was this girl named Jaclyn that I sort of fell for. And I will break up with Pricilla and see if she's interested. What do you think?"

"You're going to end an engagement for a...short term fling? That seems..."

He looked hurt now and Ava didn't know the right words she wanted to say. She had always struggled with finding the right words to say when she disagreed with something someone was doing.

"I'm sure that I don't know that whole story. I'm not one to judge", Ava told him, "you really must love this new girl and if you are sure and you pray about it then maybe it's for the best"

"She's just so mission minded", he said then, "I can learn a lot from her"

He left soon and Ava felt like he put a weight onto her. She could just sense Pricilla's hurt already and wanted to stop it somehow.

Then she ran after David and stopped him before he started talking to a group of guys.

"Maybe you should think about this some more", she said, "give it some more thought"

Then they watched as an angry Pricilla came across the property and glared at David. Who looked unsure of what was to happen next. He almost looked scared then.

"My roommate just told me that you are planning on breaking up with me? Over some girl you've only known for a few weeks? What is with this?"

Ava took a seat on a nearby bench and looked at all the drama displaying in front of her like she was watching it on TV and didn't think this seemed like Bible school.

Chapter Three

Ava watched as his fiancé gave him back his ring and walked off. She thought it was a very quick break up and she wondered if he would be sorry later.

Or even right after. Did he really think this through?

"Guess she beat me too it", he said, taking a seat next to Ava on the bench, "you have room for a pathetic guy that can't make up his mind?"

"Just focus on what you have Jaclyn. You'll go and tell her how you feel soon. She'll be happy about that I'm sure", Ava said, trying to cheer him up.

David looked at her then and didn't look away at her kind words. Ava laughed nervously then and stood, before she felt like he might kiss her.

"I should head back to my room. I still haven't met my roommate and..."

"You and I should go out sometime. I always do this though. I fall for someone and then they end things. You probably would too"

"Probably not and that's the problem", Ava said, "I really make sure that it's there with someone first before I date someone. I take my time and I'm sure that's not something that you would be willing to put up with"

He looked up at her and then waited for some other students to walk by them. Then he joined her and took a strand of hair out of her eyes, "Ava..."

"I should go. Good night", she said quickly. He followed her and laughed.

"That can't be it. You have to at least give me a reason you want to just be friends"

She stopped and faced him but it wasn't easy. It wasn't like her to like someone that she just met and now was no different.

"I just don't take chances or risks at all. Ever. I mean, besides this coming here to University.

But with you it's a bigger risk. It involves my heart. But why talk to you about this"

"You think I don't have a heart? I do. And it wants you already. Give me a chance. At least one date", he said.

"I have to go", she said, and went to leave, when he took her and kissed her. At first she loved it. Never had a guy been like that with her but she knew that it was still not wanted.

"David. I don't know you", she said, and then ran up to her room.

She sat on her bed and then went to look out the window.

She stood then and looked out the window and watched as the stars came out one by one. She then walked to the main idea where everyone hung out and then took a seat on one the benches.

She felt restless and watched as David looked at her as he checked his email at one of the computers. He looked serious then and turned back to the computer.

Ava took a seat next to him and tried to use the computer when she realized that she didn't have a password for it yet.

"You can use my computer after I'm done. I won't be long", he told her, "and I'm sorry I kissed you. I was out of line Ava. But..."

He stopped talking as more people crowded around them. Feeling uneasy Ava nodded and smiled at him, giving him a look that said how she was feeling then. And no words were needed.

"You want to go for a walk or something. It's still early. Then I can tell what I want to", he said.

She agreed and soon they were walking along the sidewalks. Then she realized what was really bothering her about them.

She knew that he still liked someone else and why was he kissing her?

"So what happened to Jaclyn?",
she asked him, "you were just
talking about her. What
happened?"

"Something happened when you
came in today. You looked
so...helpless. I just knew that that's
how I felt last year when it was my
first year and I didn't know anyone.

I wanted to make you feel
welcome here. But then as I heard
you singing I just felt like maybe
God had you here for a reason. It

doesn't always take years to realize something like that. Something special"

"Well I did feel better so thanks. I have to admit that I was a little bit disappointed when I found out that you were engaged.

And really confused if you should break up with her for someone that you just met. And now here I am, being that girl with you"

He sighed and looked at her then in a way that made her fears go away, "well, I guess everything happens for a reason. I would have found it very hard to end things with Pricilla. So maybe it's good that she ended things first"

"I guess", Ava told him, as she walked along the sidewalk and tried not to show how much she already liked him. "And you still like her?"

"Not really. We didn't have the best relationship for a while already but neither one said anything.

She's a little bit...harsh. And I'm just a big softy. I know I act tough. But really I'm just a little kid who's afraid of people hurting me"

"Well I'll try not to hurt you", she said, "I guess I'm changing things by not needing to be friends first hey? What's with me?"

He smiled at her and then stopped walking, "you mean it? So we can go on a real date sometime?"

"Yes, yes we can"

Chapter Four

Ava watched people at the
restaurant the next day at the
Restaurant where her and David
ate and tried to focus on being
herself but for some reason she felt
nervous again.

"What would you like?", he asked
her, as he opened his menu. She

looked down at the choices and then as her eyes scanned the restaurant she noticed something she did not expect. Phillip on a date...with Pricilla?

She tried not to laugh as David looked back at her and smiled warmly and then looked back at his menu.

"I took Pricilla here on our first date. I of course was crazy nervous but it began our relationship which latest a long time I guess. But I shouldn't talk about her", he said, and put down his menu and then took her hands in his.

"Let's talk about you", he said, to her fake smile. She tried not to tell him but then it became unbearable.

"There's something I should tell you. She's here, on a date...with Phillip", Ava said, to his surprise. He looked around the restaurant until his eyes fell on their table.

Ava could already tell that this wouldn't end well.

"Maybe I should have stayed home", she said to herself as she watched another event unfolding.

David confronting them and Ava couldn't believe how smug and okay with it all Pricilla looked. She wondered if this was just out of revenge then.

She didn't know what to do with herself so she left the restaurant and headed to her dorm room. It looked extra dark and extra empty then. She let a tear fall at the fact that David clearly still loved his ex-girlfriend and wondered if she was just a rebound then.

She heard the phone ring in the hallway and went to answer it then. There was static on the line and she wondered if it was David calling to apologize.

"Hello, this is the legal office of Brownlee and Camber some. We are looking for an Ava Parker. Is she available?", the women asked somewhat sternly.

"Yes, this is she", Ava answered, wondering why a legal office would want to talk to her. She waited for a moment until the women came back on.

"We have reason to believe that your birth parents are trying to reach you. They live in Texas on a ranch down there.

I work with your father and he thought that it was best that I talk to you first. He's the one that is trying to get a hold of you", she said, somewhat to Ava's surprise and confusion.

"But my father hasn't contacted me for years. Since I was six", Ava said, "why now?"

"I don't know, but he wants you to come and visit him for a week next week. Does this work for you? He can work around your schedule if you'd like"

Ava played with the phone cord and thought over her words. She like always wanted time to think and plan this trip and would she have time to see him? After all, she had classes.

"I could come for a few days", she agreed then, "but I'm in school. And maybe next week would work. Can I get back to you?"

There was a pause again, "sure, I'll give you his number"

Ava wrote down the number and then said good bye before hanging up the phone. Then she carried the piece of paper to her room and sat on her bed.

She was deep in thought as the door flew open then and reviled a loud and interesting person.

"So did I miss anything yet? Sorry I'm late. My plane was delayed a day because of bad weather. Are you my new roommate?", the girl asked her, "and why are you so upset? Someone giving you hard time already?"

Ava smiled and went to hug her hello. "It's nice to meet you. I'm Ava"

"I'm Olivia. So this is my bed then?", she said, looking around the room. "Wonderful, I was here last year too. And it seems like not much has changed around here. What's your time been like here so far?"

Ava laughed then thinking of all that had already happened there. All the fighting, kissing, new relationships, jealousy, and love.

She couldn't believe all that had gone on making her wonder what would happen next.

"It's been interesting. Already been on a date", Ava replied, sitting on her bed.

"You have already? With whom?", she wondered then, "I probably won't know him if he's a freshmen"

"It's David", Ava told her, "you know him. He was here last year too"

She took a seat on her bed and thought over if she knew him or not. Then she took out her old year book and looked for all the David's and landed on his picture.

"Oh yes. David. I remember him. He's really nice Ava. Don't let him get away", she said, "He was always nice to me last year. In fact he led worship every Sunday. What made you meet already?"

Ava blinked back surprise at her words. Could they be talking about the same person? She thought of David as someone that dated a lot of girls and here she was describing him as a gentleman. Maybe she underestimated him.

"He was practicing worship and I walked in and he invited me to join him. Then he was dating Pricilla. But they broke up", Ava described,

"You don't remember that he was dating her?"

"No, I saw them together but I didn't know they were dating. I see, well what made them break up?", she asked.

"He found someone else and then just when I thought he would date her he asked me out. It was all very confusing but he's not over Pricilla that's for sure. On our date he found her and Phillip on a date and

got really upset", Ava said, and
then realized she was gossiping.

"Well that sounds complicated.
But I know what I know and that
boy is a keeper. That's all I know",
she said, with a mystery behind her
eyes that Ava hoped that she would
begin to know what that was about.

Chapter Five

Ava packed her bags and put them into her roommate's car that she would take to go and see her parents, when she heard a knock on the door.

"David", she said, as he walked in.

"Hey, you're leaving? And I just realized something", he said, "timing hey?"

"What did you realize?", she asked.

"That it's you I want", he said, "and not any other girl. But you are going away now. Where are you going?"

"It's a long story. But I'll only be gone for a few days. And what do you mean I'm the only girl you want to be with? What about Pricilla?"

"I spent the whole time with her trying to please her when I realized I finally have something that doesn't require that much from me. I want that", he said.

She gave him an odd look, "how do you know I don't? What if I always want you to wear red? Every day"

He smiled, "then I guess red will be my new favourite colour"

"Where do you come up with the things you say? From a manual on how guys should talk to women?", she asked, "or did your mother teach you right?"

He grinned and took her in his arms. She stayed there and felt safe and happy. Why did she already know that he was comforting? There she felt like nothing could ever go wrong or hurt her.

"I'm going to see my birth parents. My dad wants to see me. I haven't actually seen them in years. I'm nervous about it. I have no idea how I'm going to get through this", she said, sitting on her bed. David looked at her and looked like he was trying to come up with the right thing to say then.

"Do you want me to come with you? For moral support? You'll need a friend out there right?", he replied, and looked vulnerable then.

"I don't know. I barely know them and it might be too soon for you to be there. I'm sorry David. I just..."

"It's fine. Things aren't official anymore are they? Our first date didn't exactly go as planned did it? I'm sorry Ava. I promise I'll make it up to you when you come back. We can go anywhere you want"

She smiled and then hugged him before she left, "thanks David. I'll miss you already. But it's only a few days"

Ava got into the car and then drove to where the road carried her to the main highway. She drove along the highway and turned on the radio to a Christian radio station.

As she pulled up to a gas station she filled up the tank and leaned against the car and thought over how this would all go.

She prayed that everything would be fine and that she would have God's peace in her as she wasn't sure if they would be happy to see her or not. Or if she would be able to give up the fact that they gave her away.

A tear fell down her cheeks as she got back into car after paying. Then she stopped beside the road and took a deep breath.

She almost went back to the school, when she looked up to see a sign that read that she was close to the next town. She decided to stay there for night and decide whether or not to go then.

She couldn't make up her mind that fast. At the hotel she sat on the bed and checked her messages on her phone. She went down the messages and then read one from David. It read,

"Dear Ava,

I miss you already", and that's all it read. She smiled though as it was exactly what she needed to read right then.

Then she went to bed and prayed about the next day. Only by God's strength could she get through this. She had many questions about why they gave her up.

But she still love them and was thankful that they had taken her to church where she grew up knowing the truth about God and how she needed him as her Savoir.

The next day Ava pulled up to her parents' house and walked up the drive way and decided that no matter how things went she would

soon be going back to school and

spending time with a boy who loved

her.

She knocked on the door and then

waited until a woman answered it.

She looked like the mother she

remembered only older and more

grey hair.

"Ava! We weren't expecting you

until tomorrow. But welcome here.

We made up the guest room

already. But feel free to sleep

anywhere", she said, "You have a good drive?"

"Yeah, I didn't know that you lived on a ranch. It's really nice here. And you have horses?", she asked, looking out over the many horses in the field.

"Yes, we have ten now. I keep wanting to sell them but your father won't let me. He loves each one like a child. Oh I shouldn't have said that. We should have tea on the veranda. I'll tell the maid that you're here", she said, "her name's Hanna. She's from England. Really nice lady. You sit on the deck and I'll be right out dear"

Ava smiled and then did as she said. But as she took a seat she couldn't help but question why they couldn't raise a daughter. She was upset that she could have grown up there.

Her mom came back and handed her a cup of tea and then took a seat next to her on a bench. Ava had many questions but wasn't sure how to ask them then. She just sat quietly and looked out over the view.

"How long have you had this ranch?", Ava asked her, and sipped her tea.

"About five years. We haven't always lived like this. But your father and I started this ranch with almost nothing and now it's grown into this. Now we can't imagine leaving it. God has blessed us"

"I still don't understand why you gave me away when I was just a child. What went so wrong? Things seemed fine when I was a child", she said.

"We didn't let you know how bad things really were. Ava, we were barely making it. We didn't have enough money to feed ourselves let alone you.

But it was the hardest decision I had to make. That's why I promised myself that when you were older I would come looking for you. I knew that I would always love you no matter what happened. We just couldn't afford to feed you"

Ava nodded and found herself almost understanding her mother's reasons. How God had worked things out anyway.

For here she was years later with a mother who loved her on a deck of a nice ranch. They could have kept her if they had known, but how could they?

Chapter Seven

The next day Ava had supper with her parents before leaving the next day.

She looked at her dad and then at her mom at the supper table and it felt strange to have a maid come in and give her the meal.

She looked down at the different forks and spoons and felt like she was at a fancy resort. She almost felt like staying there for a while longer.

"I don't want to leave tomorrow. What do I do?", she asked them. They looked back at her with hopeful expressions but not forceful.

"Stay an extra week", her mom said and passed her some more

peas. Then Ava wondered about her classes that she had just started.

"What if I come for Christmas?", she asked. "For three weeks?"

"That would work", her dad said, "Then you can stay longer and help out around here"

Her mom gave him a warning look then and Ava remembered that look from years back. How some things never changed. Even years later.

"That will be fun. I can't wait and I don't even mind if I have to help out around here. It doesn't bother me"

"So what's school like?", her dad asked, "you making all sorts of friends there?"

"Yeah, so far. I like my roommate and there's this boy that I sort of like. His name is David. But I'm not sure if it will work out yet", she explained, "but he's really nice"

After all those years her father
still looked at her in a protective
way that she almost appreciated
then. Like he would always be her
dad and nothing could ever change
that fact.

"So he's nice? Is he responsible?
Does he treat you right?", he asked,
"or can he provide for you?"

She was upset at him asking that
last one. It was the reason that
they had given her away and now
here he was wanting someone else

to look after her financially? But she held her breath and then choose her words carefully.

"I'm assuming he can, but money isn't everything. I don't need to be rich. I just want to be loved", she said, and they were quiet then.

She almost started crying then; realizing maybe her mom's reasoning wasn't so good.

"I should go to my room, where is it?"

"I'll show you", her mom said, and took her down a hallway and to a small but cute room filled with fake flowers and a note on the bed.

"We are happy to have you here", her mom told her, "and we'll miss you already as you go back to school. See you later on? We're going to a party later on at our friend's house down the road from here. It should be fun"

Ava smiled and nodded, "maybe, I'll see. Thanks...mom"

She looked emotional then and left her. Ava never guessed that she would be the real problem in this situation. She didn't expect to feel this way.

Like she had lost something so important to her. Her parents had given her a nice home for years. Why did she need more?

Ava changed into something more elegant and then walked back to the living room, ready for any fancy party she might be going to. She didn't feel comfortable until she noticed that her dad was wearing his usual jeans and flannel shirt.

"I'm ready", he said, to his wife's rolling of the eyes.

"Nice outfit dad", Ava joked, and then they all left in the car. She entered the party and looked around the room at all the very many people there.

At first she felt out of place but her mom introduced her to everyone.

"This is our daughter. She goes to University", her mom told them, "and she is taking...oh I don't even know what program you're in"

"I'm taking Nursing right now", she said, and watched as her mom was impressed but Ava tried to hide the fact that her adopted mom knew this.

She felt confused and sad now and didn't know where to go or what to do. She suddenly needed some air.

She smiled at the group of people and then walked out to the pool area. She looked back at them talking about something else quickly. And suddenly she missed her mom. Who raised her her whole life.

Ava walked to the edge of the pool and took a seat, putting her feet into the water. She looked up the stars coming out one by one and looked as a boy came and took a seat next to her.

"Hi, you looked lonely. I'm Teddy. You and I used to play together as children. You probably don't remember me hey?"

She looked at him closely and then couldn't lie. "No, I'm sorry. I guess I played with a lot of children when I was little"

"Guess so. So why are you out here and not inside being introduced to many people you don't know?", he teased.

"Needed some air. And why are you out here talking to me?", she asked him.

"I needed a break from the girls inside that like me. there's many. Not to brag or anything. But I like to find my girls", he said, eyeing her.

Ava smiled and looking at him then she suddenly had a memory of him and her playing when they were children. It was so distant

then that she just barely pictured
it.

"I remember you now", she told
him, "you were the boy that gave
me a seat on the bus on our field
trip. No one else let me sit but you
did"

"Yeah, well I was a year older so
maybe I was more mature. But I'm
glad that you finally remember me.
I wasn't sure you would"

"I do. Wow, I'm sorry I was rude earlier. I just wasn't looking for a guy right now. I was..."

"What you think I like you? I just met you", he said then, and walked back inside. Ava looked back at the pool then and then she realized that she had talked just like that to David.

How she had put him through a lot she thought. She felt like going back to the school then realizing that she already had everything that she could ever need, and

more.

Chapter Eight

Ava said good bye to her parents
and then headed on the journey
back to the school.

She would still miss them and still
planned on going back for
Christmas but she had learned so
much from being there. That God
really was all she needed. She loved

her family though and always
would.

"What happened to my siblings?",
she asked them before she left.

"Your brother Arnold is on his
own in New York, and your sister
Alice is just starting high school in
New Orleans.

They have written lately to say
how there doing. We invited them
now too but they didn't come. I
guess old wounds and such. I don't
blame them though. Please forgive

us Ava. We have learned from our mistakes", her mom told her.

Ava bit her lip and hugged her mom good bye, "I do. I long have mom. I love you and always will, it doesn't matter who I live with. You'll always be my mom"

Then she hugged her father good bye and no words were needed. Then she got into her car and drove back. She still couldn't get over her talk with Teddy.

She couldn't wait to get back to David. She had planned on dating him when she got back. Then she wondered what would happen if he didn't want her anymore? That thought was one of her biggest fears then.

As she got back to the University she ran into the chapel knowing that they would be practicing then. But there was only the rest of the group and no David. She wondered where he was then.

She practiced with the group until she noticed him walking in. Her heart beat faster as he put away his jacket and joined them.

As they sang he kept looking at her. How she wanted to talk to him. But then wasn't the time. She focused on worshipping and the words to the songs she was singing.

An hour later as practicing ended and everyone was heading back to their rooms she and David went for a walk just them. She didn't know how to bring up how she felt but as he talked the words became easier.

"So how was your time with your parents? Did you have a good time or was it hard?"

"Parts of it were good, but yeah it was hard too. But it went better than I thought. I guess I just still don't understand why they gave me away. I was already six.

What would make them do that? My mom says that it was because of money. But being there just made me realize where I was really meant to be. With you"

He smiled and his face grew red then, and she wondered what he was thinking. Did he feel the same still or did things change?

"I'm glad that you say that because things haven't changed for me at all since I kissed you. I've wanted you this whole time. Ava, I just want to know that you feel the same way I do"

"I do, I want to be with you and only you", she told him, and put her head onto his forehead as they sat on a bench. The same bench where they had first talked after Pricilla had ended things with him.

"That's good because I just want you and only you too", he said, and kissed her. Ava then smiled at him and felt better even just spending time with him again.

"So what is going on with Pricilla? What did happen when you and her talked on her date with

Phillip?", she wondered.

"Well I went to confront them and

she told me that she had every

right to move on. And that she

liked him now.

I did not expect that at all. I guess

I wasn't as over her as I thought I

was. But my head knows that we're

not right together. And my heart

needed to catch up I guess"

"Are they dating now?"

"Guess so. It doesn't really matter to me anymore. She can do what she wants. I found someone else anyway", he let her know.

"I guess you did. It's weird that I've been here for a week now and still haven't been to a class. I know I'll have some catching up to do", she said, as he walked her back to her room.

"Good night miss Ava. Have a good sleep and I'll see you tomorrow"

"Yes, but wait. About us...what are we now?", she asked, with a grin, "I mean..."

"Dating? Will you be my girlfriend?", he asked her then and took her hands in his. "Please Ava? I've waited for you as you wanted"

"Of course I will", she let him know, "and you will be my boyfriend"

He smiled and then left her and walked happily down the side walk. Ava felt happy too. She had found a love in him that she had never experienced before. Like he would be the one person in her life that wouldn't leave her and would keep loving her.

How she had waited for a love like this. A safe place to fall. That's how she felt with him. Like she had waited and waited.

After all that she had been through and all the confusion who her real family was, he was her new place to be herself.

She went to sleep that night and smiled as she changed into her pajamas and climbed into her bed. Then she closed her eyes dreaming of far off places and David, who hugged her in her dream.

Even there he was kind and gentle with her. He was the right guy for her and she would let him know just how much she really loved him.

Chapter Nine

The next day in class Ava tried to avoid Pricilla and her group of her friends that looked at her in disgust.

She was thankful when she met David later on at lunch and they took a seat at a table filled with other students.

"How was your day?", he asked

her, eating a sandwich.

"Good. But your ex-girlfriend

figured out where together now",

she replied, eating her sandwich.

"Oh, I'm sorry. She must just be

jealous. We went through a lot

together but now I'm with you", he

stated. Ava smiled but she still

wondered if they would make it.

"I know you did. It's somewhat

hard to compete with. You have all

this history and I just met you.

You'll have to tell me everything sometime. Everything about you", she said, smiling at him. Then they stopped talking as Pricilla walked past them with her group of friends.

"I'll talk to her", he said then, noticing how scared Ava looked. He tried not to laugh but she was cute and he wanted her to know that she had nothing to worry about.

"Don't worry Ava, it really will be okay. I don't like her anymore.

Really, God brought me the best

girl ever. I'm not giving you up. Not

now or anytime soon"

She faced him and took a deep

breath, "okay, but you don't need

to talk to her. I trust you"

"Good. Well I'm off. I have a

meeting with my guidance

counsellor and I need to go before

classes start again. See you later?",

he asked her, "we can go for a walk

or something?"

"Sounds good", Ava said then and watched him leave. For some reason she felt a distance between them since she got back and she wondered why that was. What happened while she was gone?

Heading to where her class was she walked by one of the classrooms and noticed David talking to a girl in the room that looked very interested in what he was saying. Then she couldn't believe her eyes as she bent over and kissed his check.

At first her blood ran cold and then she took the stairs out of the school and ran to her dorm room. Her thoughts were scattered then.

At first she felt in denial, that she didn't see anything. Then she thought that they were probably just friends. Then she thought that she would just forgive him and they could still work things out.

But the ache in her heart made her think again. She felt like going home, but she didn't know which one. Then she found herself knowing what she needed to do.

She went to where her roommate was and asked her if she could use her car. Once she agreed, Ava drove and drove. Until she reached her parents place.

She opened the door without knocking and lay on the couch. Tears fell down her face and she still had the image in her mind.

She felt heartbroken and alone.

What could help her now?

Falling asleep, her mom walked in

and found her laying there. She put

one of the blankets over her and

then went back to bed. For some

reason it didn't seem odd to her to

have her there.

Even the next morning as she

made her coffee and pancakes it

felt normal. The ranch seemed to

hold a new air like it was spring or

a new season. Of all the hurts that Ava had gone through in her life she had to admit as she ate breakfast, her parents weren't one of them.

"You look like you were crying", her mom told her, "did something happen at the school?"

"I saw a girl kissing the guy I had just started dating. While she just kissed his cheek but they may as well have been kissing. I can't believe it"

They were quiet as her dad came
in from working the ranch and then
he was quiet as they looked at him.
He rubbed his chin.

"Something on my face?"

"You're daughter has been hurt by
a boy. Give her some advice. I'll be
feeding the horses and I'll be back.
Be nice honey"

"I'm always nice and what boy?
The boy that you were talking
about at school?"

"Yes, and I'm not going back", Ava said, "I'm staying here"

"That's not my daughter to quit once she starts something. I remember that about you even as a child. I would ask you to come from the park and you said, no way dad. I'm staying here", he said, with a grin.

"That was the park and I was young then. I don't want to go back", she said, "I don't have what it takes to be a nurse either"

"Yes you do. I see the same drive in you that I have. You'll be a good nurse. So some guy hurt you, you stand your ground and hold your head up high. If God is for you, who can be against you?"

She thought over his words and smiled. "Maybe I'll go next year and take this year off. Work with you here"

"Fine. I need some help around this time of year. But you promise me that you won't give up"

"I promise", she told him, "thanks dad"

"Anytime. Now some coffee and then more work", he said, making some coffee. "If you want, you can help your mother with the horses"

Ava smiled and then watched her mom and dad later as they talked while fixing a fence post.

How her heart was happy in that moment. She hadn't expected it but she had to admit that being there made her happy. Maybe everything

happened for a reason, she
thought.

She drank her coffee and flipped
open a magazine looking at all the
new outfits in style then. When she
went to help her parents with the
ranch.

She fed the horses and smiled as
she stroked his mane. How pretty
and black that horse was. She
almost didn't miss being at the
school anymore.

"What's his name?", she asked.

"Sparky. He was our first horse here. And she's the prettiest if you ask me", she heard someone behind her say then. She met eyes that she knew, and knew well.

"Teddy", she said, meeting his gaze, "what are you doing here?"

"I work here", he said, taking the pail from her and feeding the horse. She almost didn't like him just taking over. But she guessed he was used to it by now.

"You remember Teddy? You used to play together as kids", her dad said, "he's worked with us now for two years"

"That's why you talked to me the other day", she said, figuring it all out, "makes sense"

"That and you were the prettiest girl there", he said, to her parent's surprise. They soon left and Ava was alone with Teddy and she didn't know what to say then.

"You want to ride? There's a path I like to take. I can show it to you if you want", he said, handing her the reigns.

"I don't know, I mean, you just met me...again. It might be too soon", she teased him, "isn't that what you told me?"

He smiled and then watched as she saddled him up and they went riding. Ava and he rode along the path which led to a clearing and a lake. The open fields and valleys made her so thankful for her relationship with God and she wanted more than ever to grow in her faith.

"I just can't believe how pretty it really is here", she said, "It was all created"

"Yup. God knew what he was doing", he said, "it never gets old or tiring does it? Still as pretty as ever here. I've known him for years now"

"I have too", she said, and their eyes met. She then raced him back to the ranch and they took the horses back to the barn. Then she raced him inside.

"I always win", she teased, "next time I'll let you win"

He grinned and winked at her before they sat down for supper with her parents. Ava loved how things turned out differently then she thought they would. But even better then she had planned.

Chapter Ten

In the weeks that followed Ava went through more ups and downs. She went through text messages from David trying to excuse what she saw.

She went through more awkward talks with her parents. She went through kisses with Teddy and time alone with God.

But what she loved the most was knowing that God would look after her and take care of her like he always had.

She never needed to doubt his love and he way that he created her and loved all the little things about her.

She felt cherished and loved more than ever. Without great expectations or "needing to do's", she felt...free. Free in Christ and who he was changing her into.

She walked to the barn one August afternoon and saddled up one of the horses and took it across the field and along the river where she rode with Teddy.

Then she met him down by the river and he was fishing. He looked somewhat bored until he noticed her. His eyes lit up and he helped her down the slope.

"Catching anything?", she asked, "and can you teach me how?"

His eyes lit up, "I can show you but then you'll soon be better at everything then I am. I can't have that can I?"

"I promise that I'll be so bad at it. And I'll have no idea how to ride now either", she said, seriously until she began to laugh. He flirted back and then she found herself in his arms then.

At first she back away until he kept holding her. So she stayed right there. She also didn't let go of the feeling that was beginning in her.

"Teddy. Do you ever plan on leaving here? Like you must have dreams and goals. Do you want to go to school or something? Like college?"

"When? Today? Today I want to stay right here...with you. Why would I go anywhere? I finally found you. Ava...I know that you've been hurt so I've been patient. But I want...never mind"

"You want what?", she asked, "because we've been friends for a while now. Is that all you want?"

"Right now? I want to fish", he said to her disappointment. "But I think that sometime we should talk about us"

Her eyes lit up then and she took a deep breath, "so how do you do this?"

He showed her how to fish as she watched him do it. Then she tried it and the hook found a nearby tree and hooked into it. Ava laughed and Teddy looked annoyed at first and then laughed too.

"This reminds me of teaching my little cousins", he teased, "They were better though"

Ava shook her head, "hey. My parents pay you. You have to be nice to your boss' daughter"

"Oh, is that so?", he said, looking at her. Then he kept fishing as she headed back to help feed the horses. She walked and then looked back to where he stood.

He looked somewhat vulnerable and lonely then. Making her turn back and join him again.

For some reason they were finding someone in each other that she was growing to appreciate. And her appreciation was growing. It was growing and she didn't stop it.

"You should show me again", she said, "I will get the hang of this. I have always wanted to do this and now I will"

He took her fishing rod and at first he was going to show her how. When he realized something.

"You don't really care do you? You just want an excuse to be with me. Because we can do something else too"

"Like what?", she asked, looking at him.

Then he reached over and kissed her. "That"

She smiled and nodded. "That's good too. But I really do want to fish"

The two of them fished until she finally caught something and then they kissed the fish and set it free. Back into the water. Then they watched as it swam away.

"Bye fishy", Ava said to Teddy's smile. Then they headed back to the ranch, hand in hand.

"I guess we should tell my parents about us", she told him, "they might wonder something's"

"Then they'll think they had something to do with it", he said, "but I want to take you out on a real date Ava. A restaurant or something"

Suddenly she had flashbacks to her time with David and how he used to say something's like that. "How about we just watch a movie at my place?"

"Sounds good", he said, "I do like you though"

"I like you too. And I think I always will", she said, as they entered the house and joined her parents.

They sat down to eat supper and she found herself looking at Teddy as though he was the one that she just might marry someday. On her journey. Ava's journey.

The End

Printed in Great Britain
by Amazon

34100649R00078